Pig Pig Meets the Lion

David McPhail

iái Charlesbridge

For my darlin' Adeline, with love from Papa Dave

Published by Charlesbridge
85 Main Street
Watertown, MA 02472
(617) 926-0329
www.charlesbridge.com

Library of Congress Cataloging-in-Publication Data
McPhail, David, 1940–
Pig Pig meets the lion / David McPhail.
p. cm.
Summary: A friendly lion escapes from the local zoo, and Pig Pig wants to
keep him.
ISBN 978-1-58089-358-9 (reinforced for library use)
1. Swine—Juvenile fiction. 2. Lion—Juvenile fiction.
3. Friendship—Juvenile fiction. 4. English language—Prepositions—Juvenile fiction.
5. Picture books for children. [1. Pigs—Fiction. 2. Lion—Fiction.
3. Friendship—Fiction. 4. English language—Prepositions—Fiction.] I. Title.
PZ7.M478818Pim 2012
813.54—dc22   2011009031

Printed in China
(hc) 10 9 8 7 6 5 4 3 2 1

Illustrations done in pen and ink and watercolor on Arches paper
Display type and text type set in Goudy
Color separations by KHL Chroma Graphics, Singapore
Manufactured by Regent Publishing Services, Hong Kong
Printed September 2011 in Shenzhen, Guangdong, China
Production supervision by Brian G. Walker
Designed by Susan Mallory Sherman

Pig Pig had quite a surprise when he woke up that morning.

He jumped **out** of bed . . .

and ran **down** the stairs.

Pig Pig and the lion dashed **into** the kitchen.

"A lion escaped from the zoo," Pig Pig's mother said.

"I know," said Pig Pig as he dove **under** the table.

Pig Pig raced **across** the living room.

He climbed **atop** the big chair.

The lion climbed **up,** too . . .

but the chair tipped **over.**

The lion wanted to sit **beside** Pig Pig.

It was too crowded, so Pig Pig jumped **off.**

"Hey, look! The lion is **on** the TV!" Pig Pig said.

"Oh, that's nice," answered Pig Pig's mom from **inside** the kitchen.

The lion leaped **through** the air . . .

onto Pig Pig.

"If I found the lion," Pig Pig called to his mother, "could I keep him?"

"I'm afraid not, dear," Pig Pig's mother answered. "The lion belongs in the zoo. Besides, we already have a cat."

"Could we visit the lion at the zoo?" asked Pig Pig.

"Of course we could, dear," said his mother.

"As often as you like."